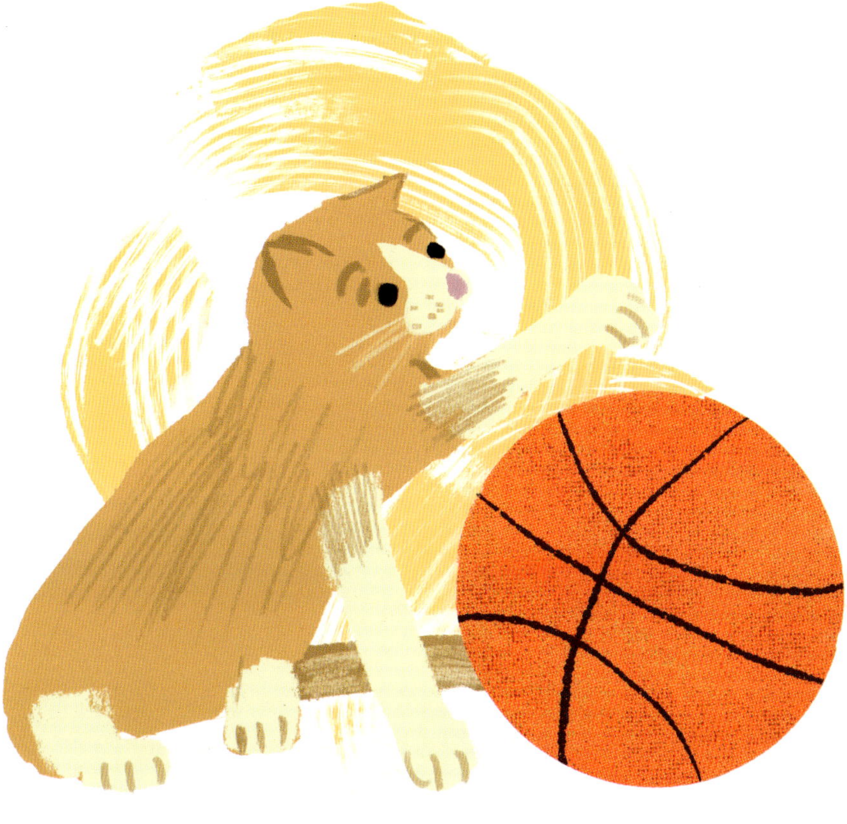

This book is for every woman and girl who has ever been told to behave or not to take up space. And, of course, to my mother and grandmother who showed me how to be brave. — CA

For my mom, the BRAVEST woman I know. — AM

Text copyright © 2025 by Chantaie Allick
Illustrations copyright © 2025 by Aaron Marin

Tundra Books, an imprint of Tundra Book Group,
a division of Penguin Random House of Canada Limited

All rights reserved. The use of any part of this publication reproduced, transmitted in any form or by any means, electronic, mechanical, photocopying, recording, or otherwise, or stored in a retrieval system, without the prior written consent of the publisher — or, in case of photocopying or other reprographic copying, a license from the Canadian Copyright Licensing Agency — is an infringement of the copyright law.

Please note that no part of this book may be used or reproduced in any manner for the purpose of training artificial intelligence technologies or systems.

Library and Archives Canada Cataloguing in Publication

Title: Amoya Blackwood is brave / written by Chantaie Allick and illustrated by Aaron Marin.
Names: Allick, Chantaie, author. | Marin, Aaron, illustrator.
Identifiers: Canadiana (print) 20240335821 | Canadiana (ebook) 20240335880 | ISBN 9781774881590 (hardcover) | ISBN 9781774881606 (EPUB)
Subjects: LCGFT: Picture books. | LCGFT: Fiction.
Classification: LCC PS8601.L553 A81 2025 | DDC jC813/.6—dc23

Published simultaneously in the United States of America by
Tundra Books of Northern New York, an imprint of Tundra Book Group,
a division of Penguin Random House of Canada Limited

Library of Congress Control Number: 2024934199

Edited by Samantha Swenson
Designed by Sophie Paas-Lang
Production edited by Katelyn Chan
The artwork in this book was created with acrylic paint, collaged paper and water-soluble crayon and edited digitally.
The text was set in Gumbo.

Printed in China

www.penguinrandomhouse.ca

1 2 3 4 5   29 28 27 26 25

AMOYA BLACKWOOD IS BRAVE

written by
Chantaie Allick

illustrated by
Aaron Marin

tundra

Amoya Blackwood was brave.
She was loud, bold and carefree —
a bit of a know-it-all too.

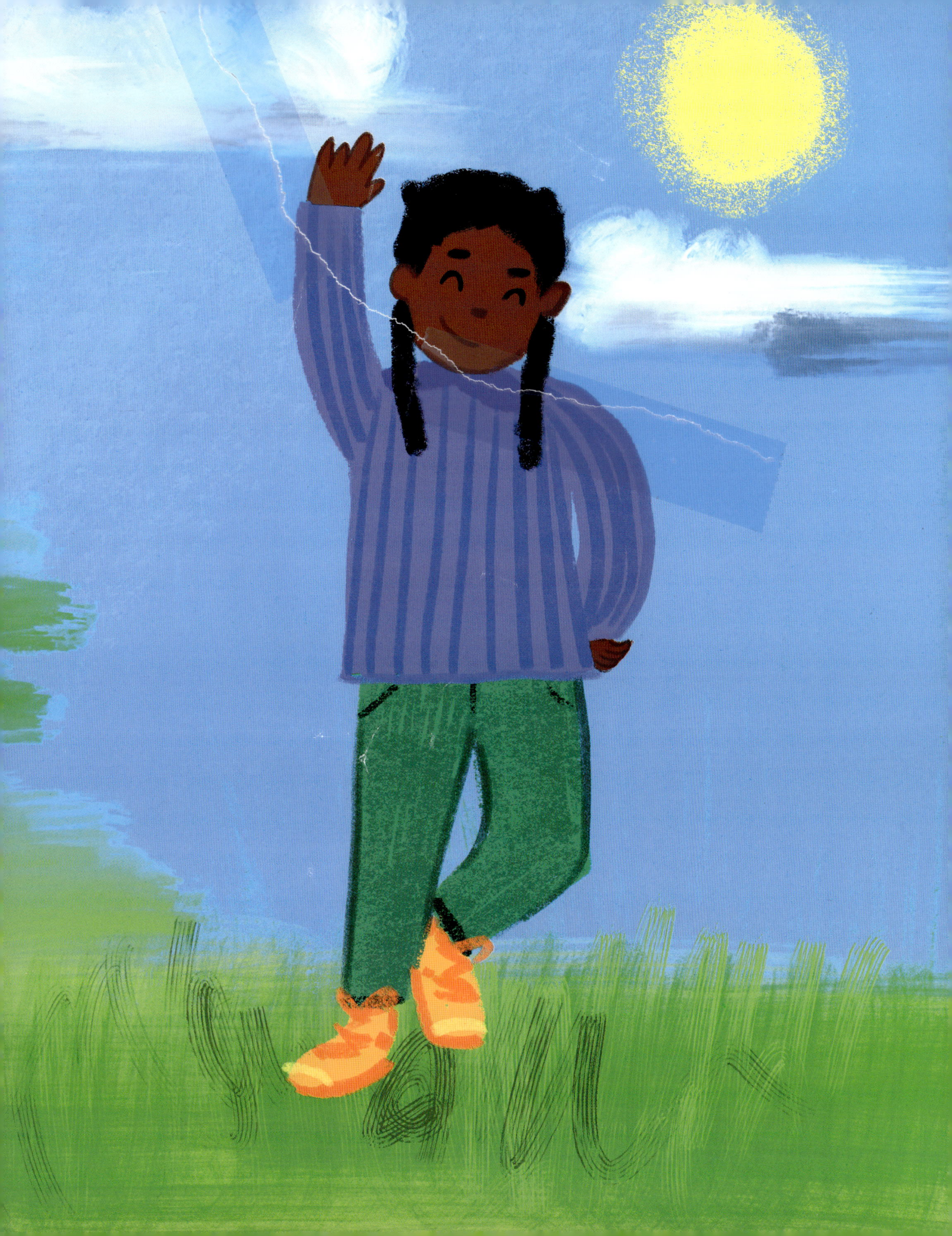

She always had the answer in class.

And knew just what to say to make her friends laugh.

She sang loudly in choir,
though she was a bit off-key.

**And while she wasn't the best,
she danced with total and utter glee.**

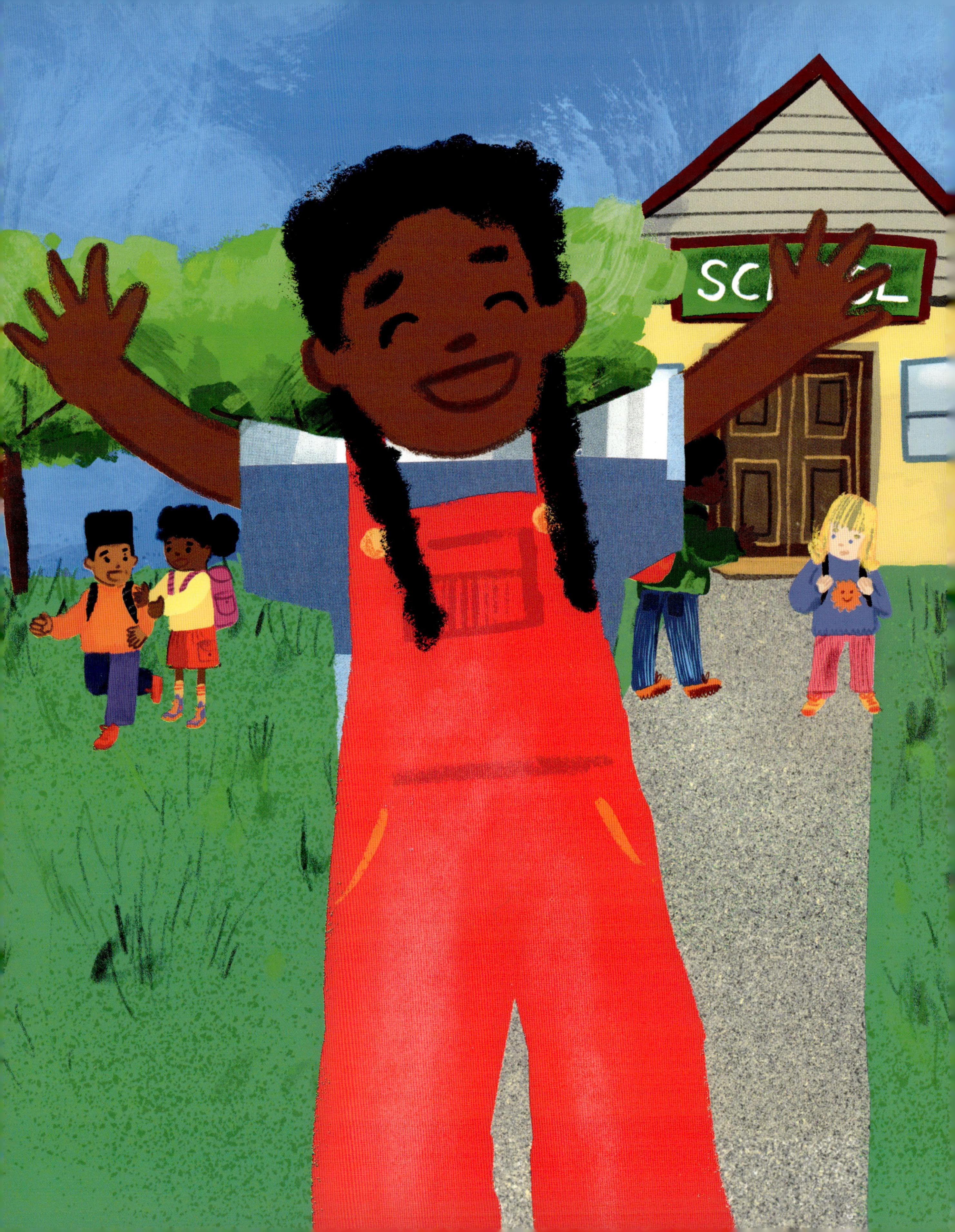

Amoya Blackwood showed up each day with a big bright smile on her face.

Amoya Blackwood entered a room and always took up space.

But then one day, Amoya happened
to see a certain look on the faces
of adults less carefree.

Be quiet, they said,
and she listened, not singing
as loudly in choir.

Calm down, they said,
and she listened, not dancing
as freely on stage.

Don't show off, they said,
and she listened, not raising
her hand in class.

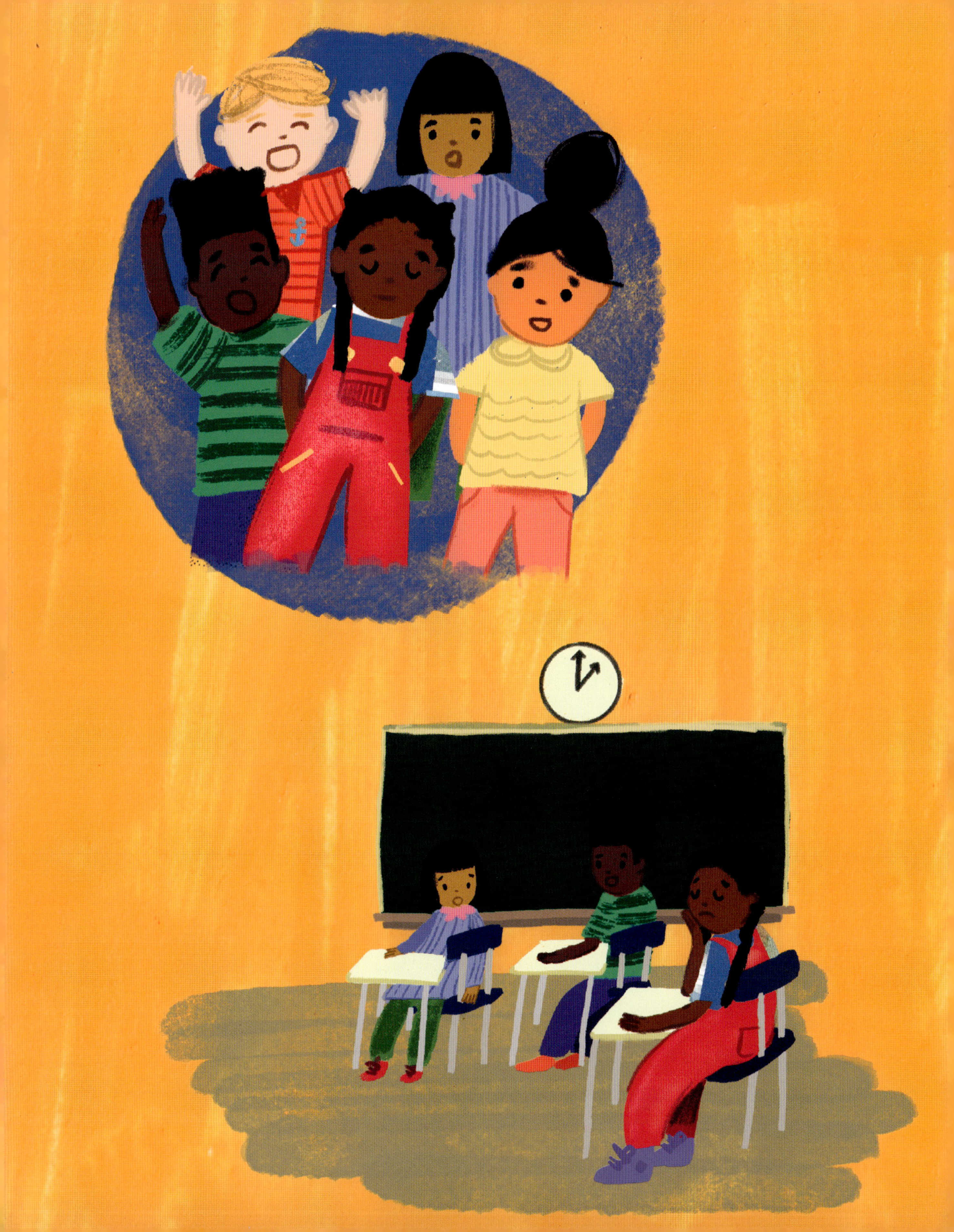

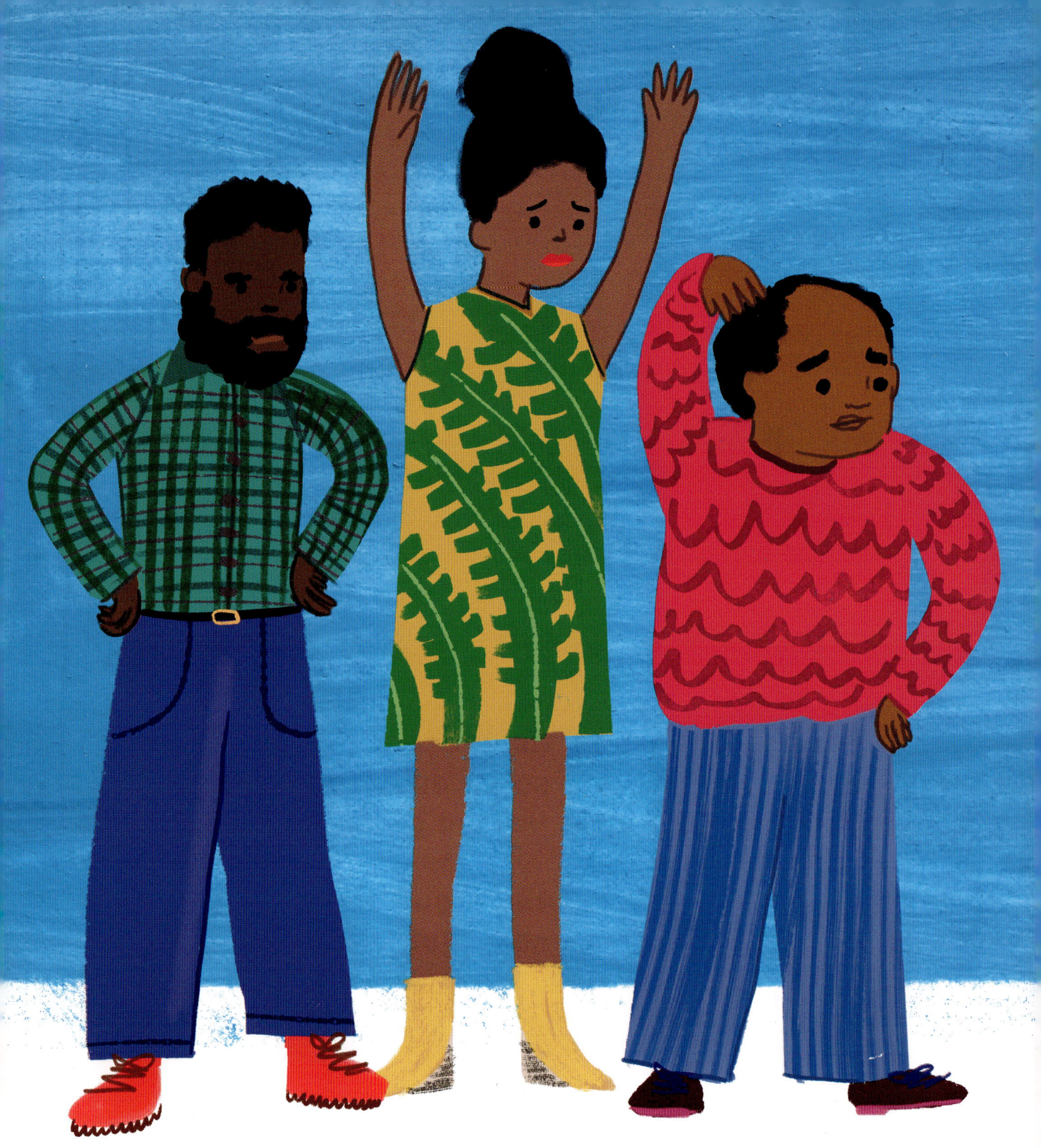

They wanted Amoya to shine less, and Amoya paid attention.

But every time she did what they said and hid that magical light that was her,

Amoya Blackwood shrank.

She got smaller and smaller and smaller, until one day you could see that Amoya Blackwood was different.

She was no longer loud, bold or carefree.

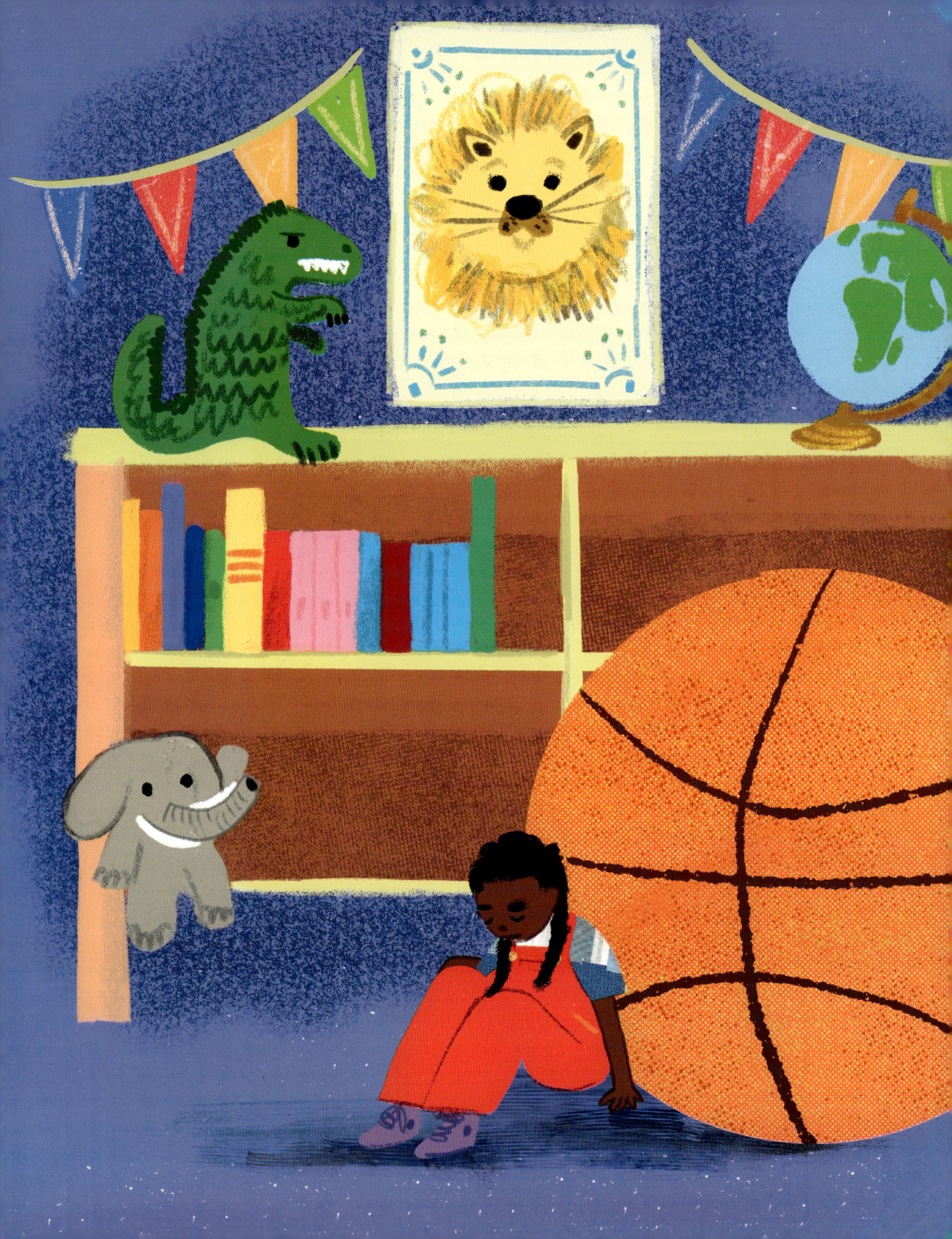

In fact, Amoya was now the smallest she had ever been.

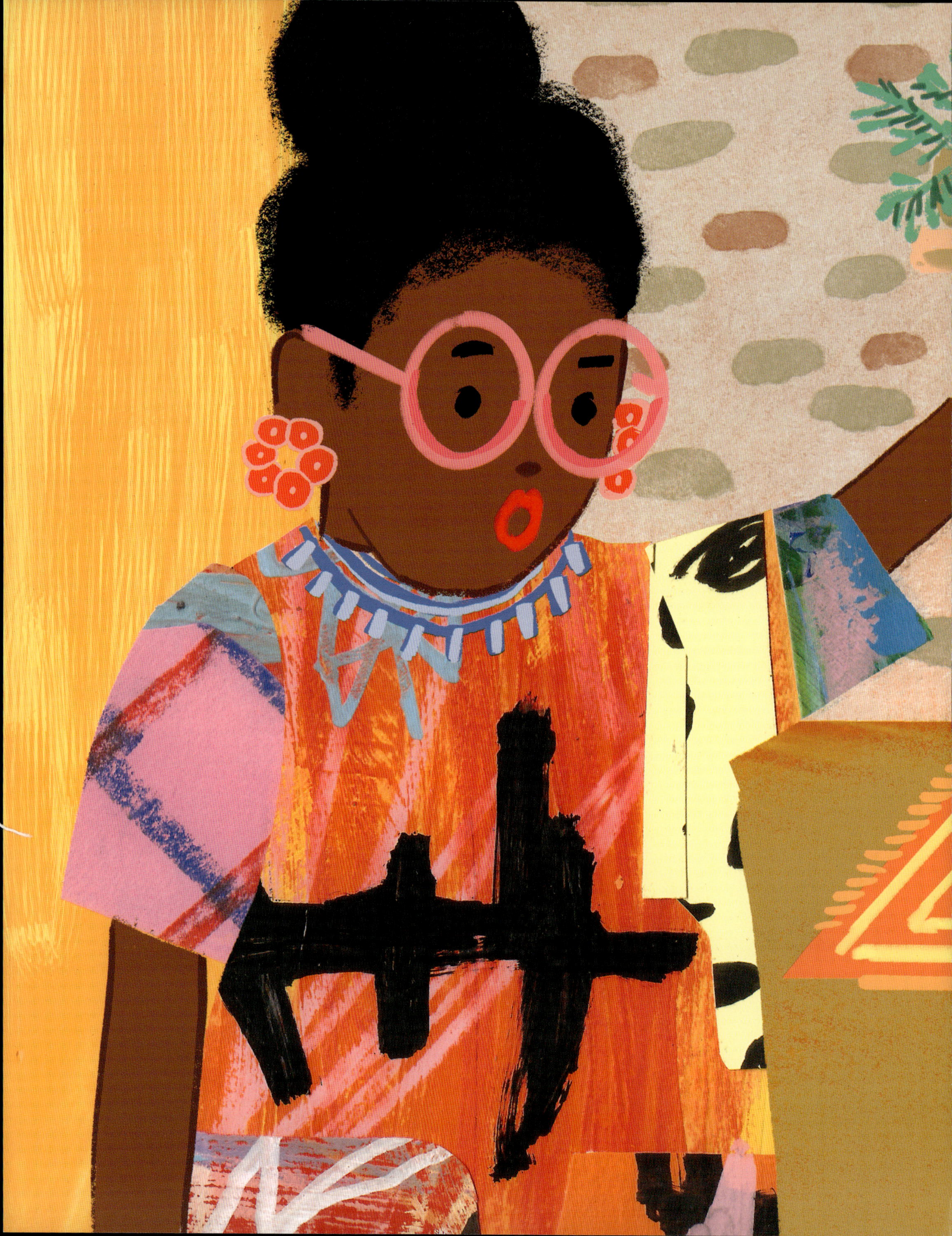

"What happened to you?" her gran asked one day.

And that made Amoya shrink even more,
but from sadness this time because her gran
was the one who'd taught Amoya to stand tall.

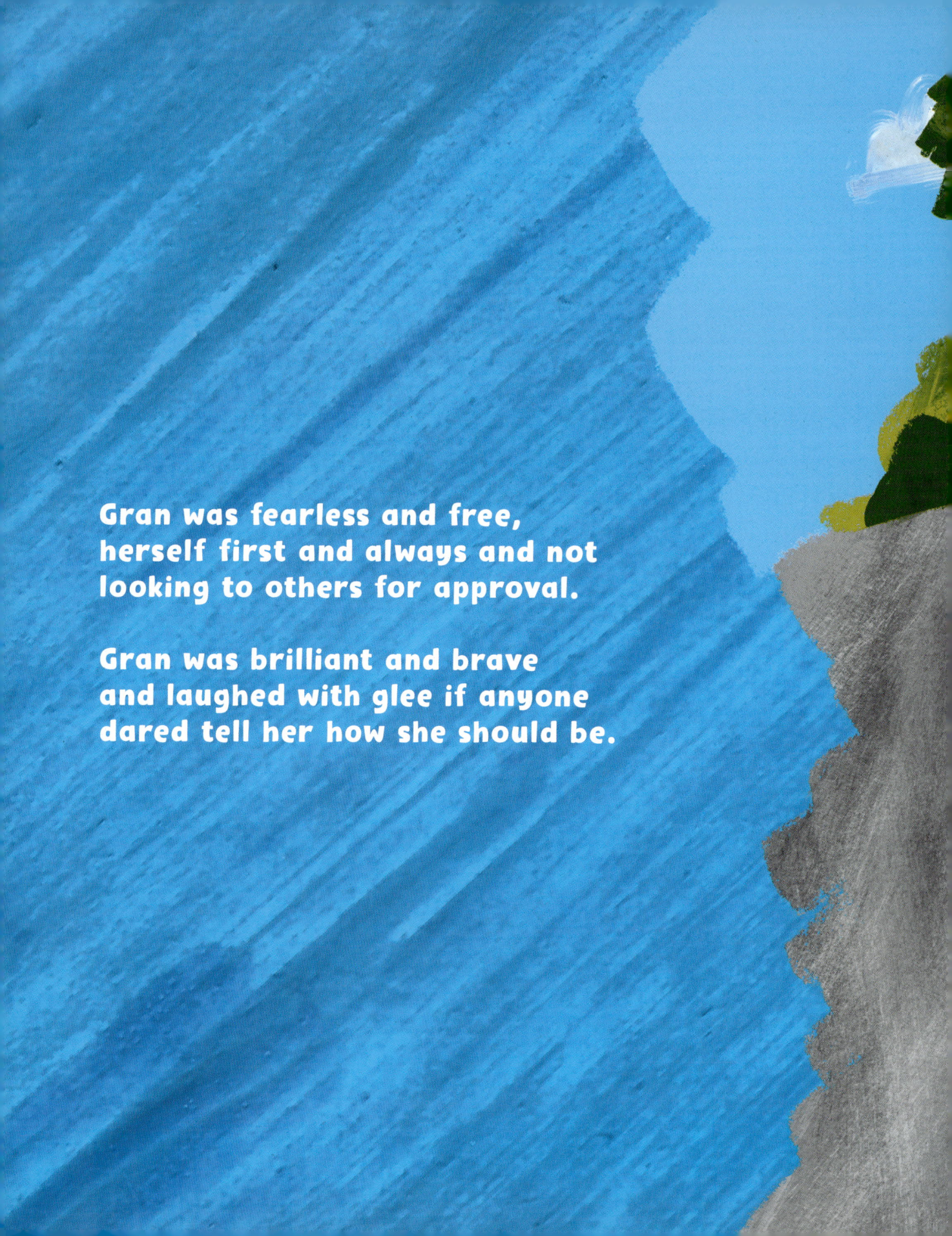

Gran was fearless and free,
herself first and always and not
looking to others for approval.

Gran was brilliant and brave
and laughed with glee if anyone
dared tell her how she should be.

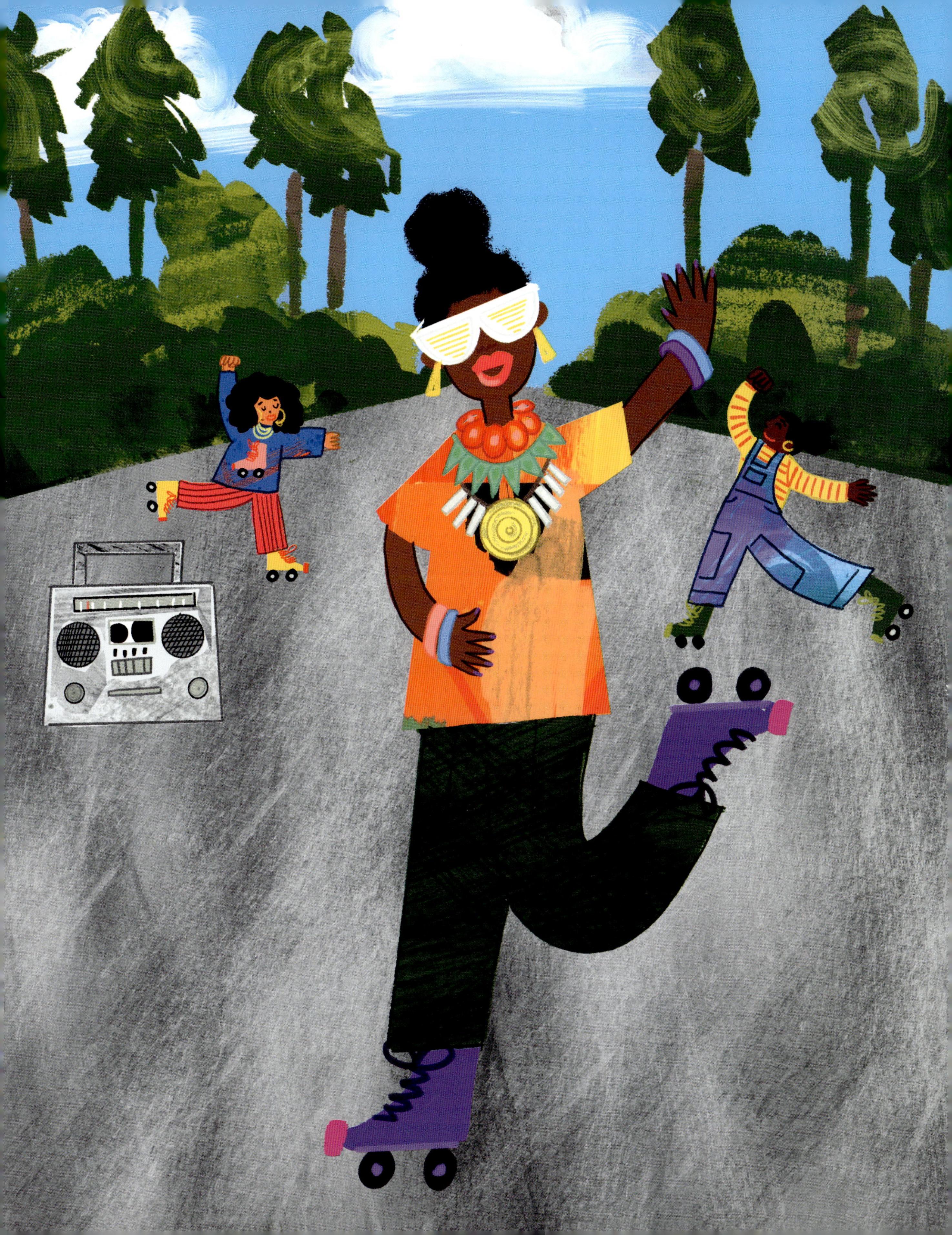

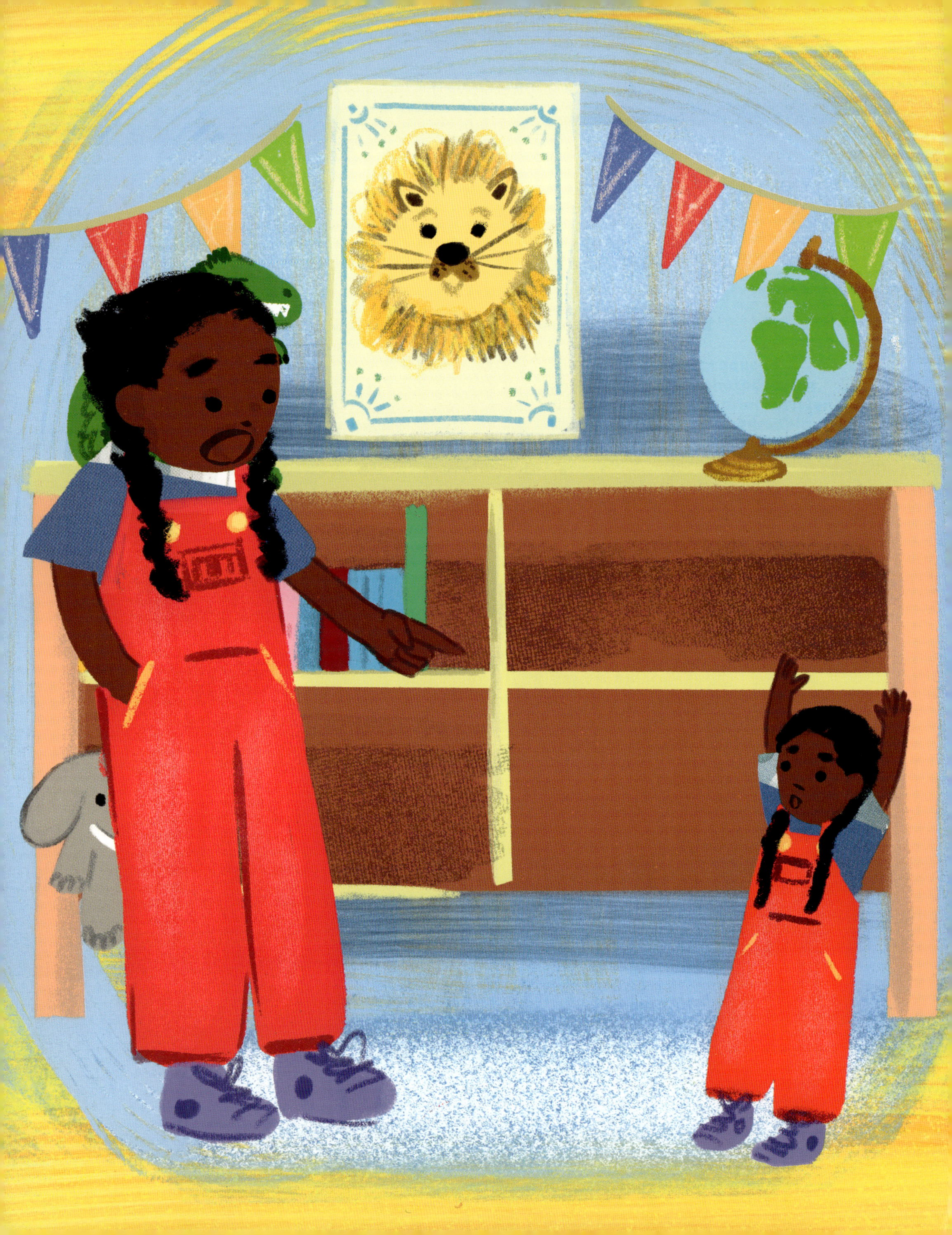

In her rush to fit in and please the people around her, Amoya had stopped looking up to those who stood tall.

"What happened to you?" she asked herself too, missing the Amoya she'd left behind.

She couldn't believe how small she'd become as she hid who she was meant to be.

But Amoya Blackwood was still brave, no matter how small she was now.

So she took a deep breath, gave her gran a hug and decided to make a change.

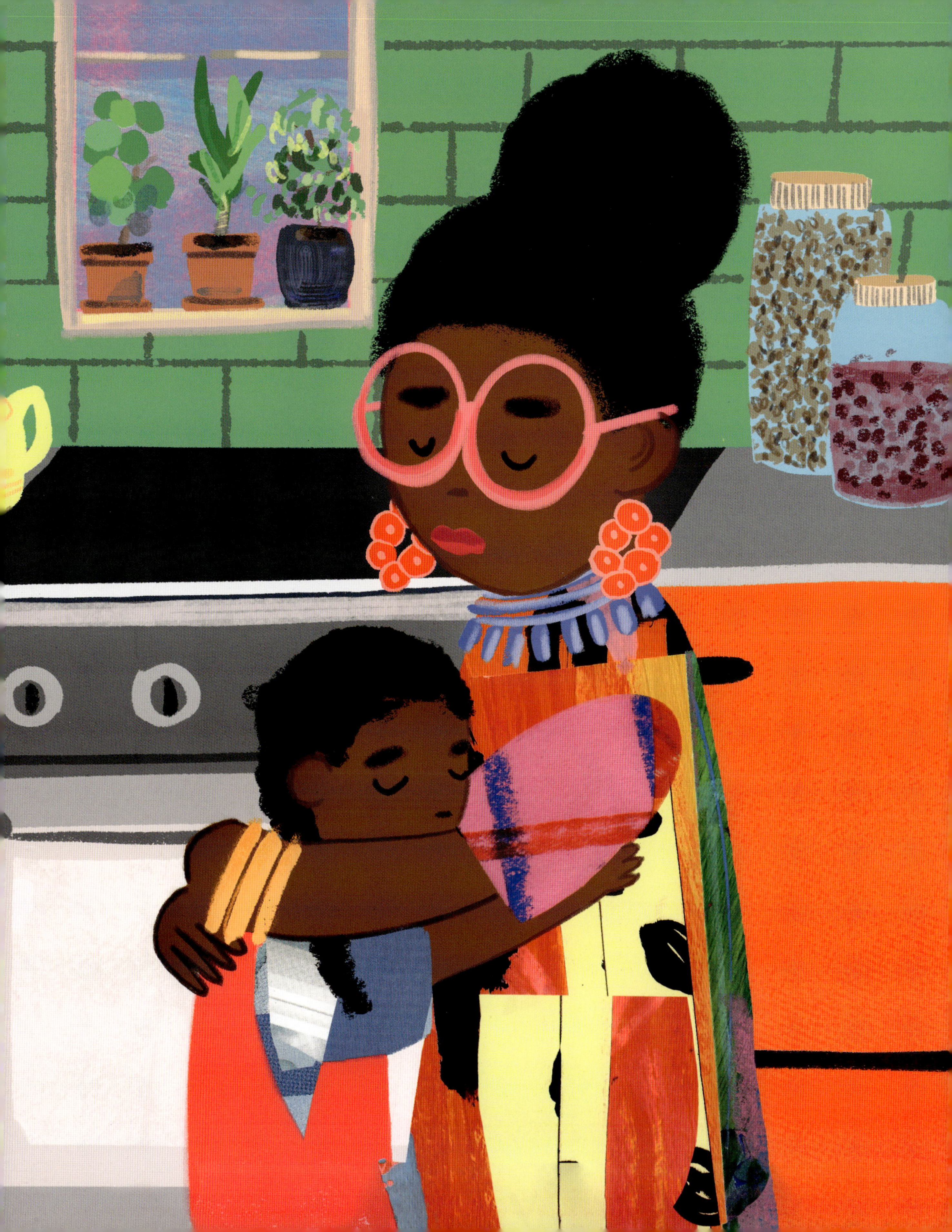

She sang loudly in choir again and answered all the questions in class.

She danced as if the world were her stage and made her friends giggle and laugh.

Amoya Blackwood was brave, ignoring anyone who wanted her to be small.

Amoya Blackwood was a light shining bright, unwilling to hide it at all.

And with each act of bravery, each small show of self, Amoya Blackwood grew.

She got taller and taller and taller, until one day Amoya became the tallest she'd ever been.

She stood so tall and brave, herself first and always, that she inspired the people around her.

They danced more freely and sang loudly, even if they weren't the best. They shone bright and bold in all of their glory with no hint of fear at all.

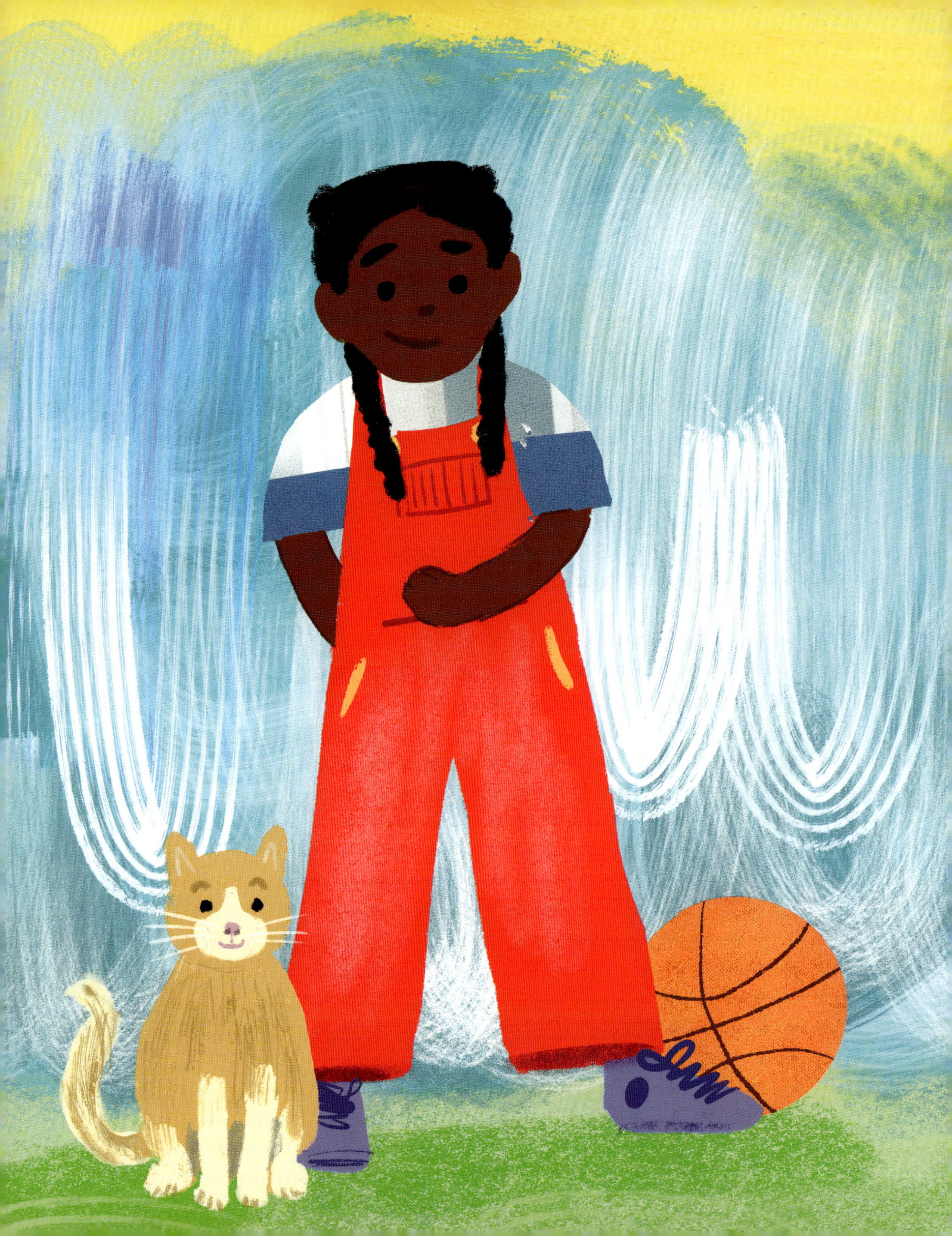

Because there's something magical in Amoya and you, too, when you choose the bravery of just being you.

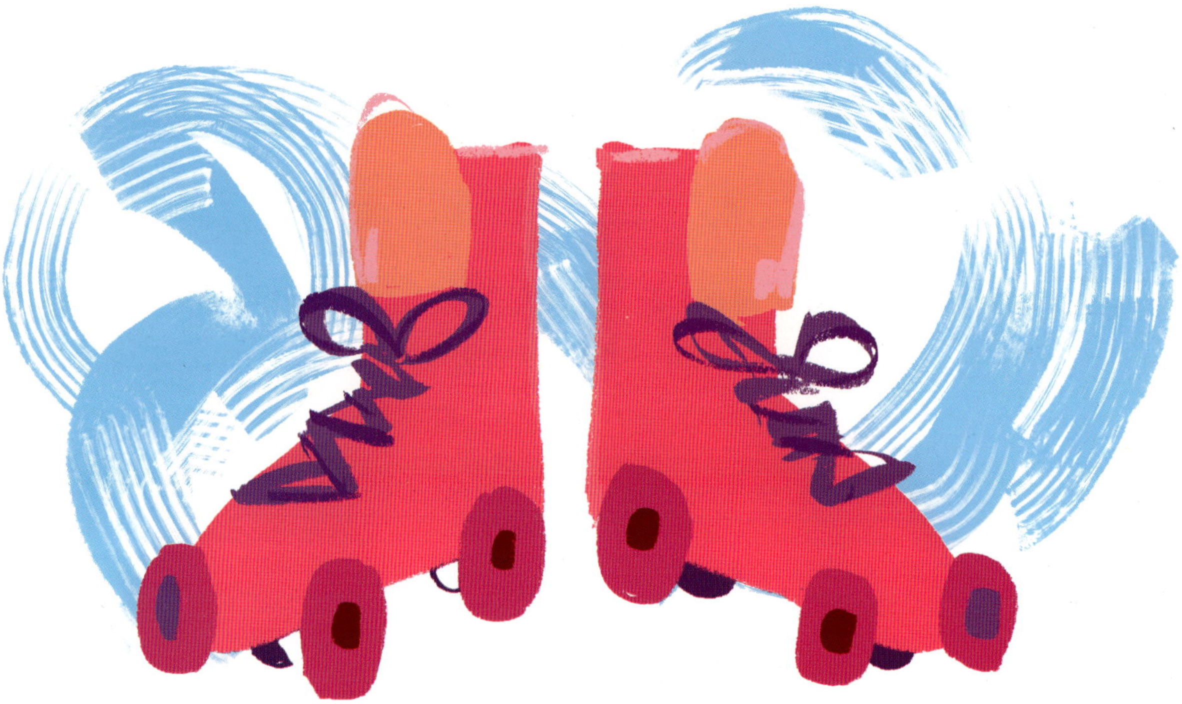